THE HAND IN THE WELL

SEBASTIAN BARKER

The Hand in the Well

Sebastian Barker

ENITHARMON PRESS LONDON
1996

AUTHOR'S NOTE

My thanks to the editors of the following, in which some of the poems were first accepted for publication: *The Rialto, Acumen, Chapman, Lines Review, London Miscellany, Orbis, The Swansea Review, New Statesman and New Society, Touching the Sun* (Hearing Eye, 1995), *Completing the Picture* (Stride Publications, 1995), and *Norman MacCaig: A Celebration* (Chapman, 1995).

My special thanks to The Royal Literary Fund.

First published in 1996
by the Enitharmon Press
36 St George's Avenue
London N7 0HD

Distributed in Europe
by Password (Books) Ltd.
23 New Mount Street
Manchester, M4 4DE

Distributed in the USA and Canada
by Dufour Editions Inc.
PO Box 7, Chester Springs
PA 19425, USA

© Sebastian Barker 1996

ISBN 1 870612 22 1

The front cover image is reproduced
by kind permission of Patrick Caulfield
and Waddington Galleries Ltd.

Typeset in 10pt Bembo by Bryan Williamson, Frome,
and printed in Great Britain by
The Cromwell Press, Broughton Gifford, Wiltshire

CONTENTS

The End of the World   7

I.   **TINKERING WITH THE FINE TUNING**
New Words on the High Wire   9
Tinkering with the Fine Tuning   10
The Hand in the Well   11
The Ruined Tower   12
The Tractor   13
Sun-Pig   14
The Constructed Castle   15
A Visit to the Village   16
A Simple Twist of Fate   17
Kristel   18
Go, Gracious Words   19

II.   **THE LIGHT ON THE RIVER**
A Monk Arrives   21
Church Bells   21
The Iron Gang   21
Against Seriousness   22
Fête   22
People   22
The Friend Who Is   23
Bowler Hat   23
Poetry   23
Vega   23
Justice   24
Double Take   24
The Light on the River   24

III.   **IN THE CRADLE OF THE POETS**
In the Cradle of the Poets   25
In Praise of Périgord   26
St Agne (In Defiance of an Abstraction)   27
Visitation in the Mountains   28
A Glass to Nature: On a Friend's Sixtieth Year   29
Norman MacCaig   30
Daughter   31
Spring Day near Reepham   31
A Week in the Country   32
The Mystery of Wine   33
Immortal Jellyfish   34
A Sealed Box for Xanthi   35

IV. BESTIAL
    Sow   37
    Piglet   38
    Moorhen   38
    Fly   38
    Butterfly   39
    Mandril   39
    Moving House   39
    Soloist   40
    Hunting Owl   40
    Heifer   40
    Pikes   41

V. A LOVE SONG TO EROS
    I Saw Him in my Sleep Last Night   43
    Dalliance   44
    Picnic   44
    Entente Cordiale   44
    Memo   45
    A Game of Croquet   45
    Perfect Form   45
    Homelife Study   46
    Muse   46
    Strike the Lovely Dumb   47
    Undone by Love   48
    Drinking Song   49
    A Love Song to Eros   50

VI. THE DANCING CROCODILE
    Grief   51
    Being Here. Two Poems for Adam Johnson (1965-93)   52
    The Cause   53
    The Wicked Corkscrew   54
    Remorse   55
    The Thin End of the Wedge   56
    Sister   57
    The Wild Men   58
    The Sage of the Cambrian Mountains   59
    The Dancing Crocodile   60
    The Ballad of Human Sacrifice   61
    The Ratchet Effect   63

THE END OF THE WORLD

I came to the end of the world.
For some time, I knew,
Things had been getting too serious.
Then, from the void outside existence,
Came the sound of Greeks laughing.

Dedicated to Hilary Davies

*

'This is the money-get, mechanic age.'
Ben Jonson

I

Tinkering with the Fine Tuning

NEW WORDS ON THE HIGH WIRE

At last the time has come when I can speak.
You think I cannot speak? Detect the lies?
The prospect before me is categorically bleak.
And shall I look on that, as the larks arise?

They come in the morning (see, my death's head pales)
And sing, like Mozart, with so clear a voice,
I grow sick of looking in my green entrails,
And view, like justice, the razor's edge of choice:

Sweet pity held me, in a long embrace;
Compassion took me, like love itself on fire;
But this is richer, tantamount to grace,

The cutting edge of language, as it hurls me higher.
And on the heights, I walk immortal space,
With death below, new words on the high wire.

TINKERING WITH THE FINE TUNING

Ever since I came here
People have been asking me,
Why don't I join in
Tinkering with the fine tuning?

None of them, it must be said,
Is anything less than exemplary,
As the brass armatures and copper coils
Indicate to the initiated.

In time, thank goodness,
I get over my embarrassment.
They, too, are grateful
I no longer set them on edge.

All week long, as they labour
With their scalpels, pipettes, and microscopic
Soldering-irons, I sit reading a book
On the social functions of human sacrifice.

By now I am irritated.
Why did they ask me to come?
So I stroll over and put the boot in
The fine tuning, demanding to know

What they think they are doing?
We were on the verge, they have the audacity to say,
Of tuning in to the human heart,
Until you came along. Read this, I say.

THE HAND IN THE WELL

Sunlight tumbled into the well
Where the children were gazing.
A dropped pebble confirmed
The water was deeper than their worst suspicions.

Why was it, the doctors asked,
A hand reached from the depths
And dragged one of them in
To be lost forever?

Many years later, going his rounds
In the city institution,
A wise old bird, long used to the caprice
Of the insane, came across the boy,
Now wrinkled and grey and somewhat overweight.

The well is before me now,
No more and no less real.
Around it the doctors gather,
Too canny to peer in, muttering
Like the children who got away.

THE RUINED TOWER

It is scarcely visible from the road.
A dark outline, tall and perpendicular,
Trembles in the trees, as if unlooked at
For years. Once under the trees,
A thick matting of ivy hides most of it,
Though a half-collapsed doorway mouths a spiral stair
Of dubious stone. Something warned us
Not to set foot inside, but being carefree,
A young couple on holiday,
There seemed no point in worrying.

People tell of the ruined tower
As a place not unduly haunted,
Even if only because, they insist,
It is
A fairy tale, a legend, a mythological freak.

But, at night, when the moon is behind the branches,
Its outline appears in their minds,
A dark outline, tall and perpendicular,
Trembling in the trees. And always we
Disappear through the doorway, climbing the stair
To fall to our deaths
Beneath a quiet thunder of masonry.

Some say our tale
Is an allegory of marriage
Doomed by antique laws
To a fatal end.
But the wise ones know
The ruined tower exists
Both in and out of the mind
Consuming youth with inexhaustible appetite.

THE TRACTOR

All day the people laughed
Because of the success of the harvest.
Even the wine-vats
Pretended a little jollity.
But under the frown of the tractor
The future waited.

Contrary to expectation,
Harvest after harvest
Failed. Distant relatives returned
Over the withered valleys.
Grimness ticked in the prettiest lips,
As the people began to die.

Only the tractor,
Obdurate beyond reason,
Laughed at the crop failures,
Laughed at the earth dug from the newborn graves,
A black jelly of laughter under the winter moon.

It laughed at the idiocy of man,
The pride and the hubris.
It laughed at the utter dependence on God.
It laughed at the future and the harvests
That were yet to be.

SUN-PIG

A pig rolls out of the sun
And lands, four-square, on my lawn.
His eyes are bright and the curl on his tail
Both questions and jokes about my existence.

But then the great archer
Bestrides our petty encounter,
As the bow is drawn back
And the arrow aimed.

Only the blood
Dripping from my sun-pig
Indicates the dignity
With which I grieve.

THE CONSTRUCTED CASTLE

Oh yes it stood
On the rock above the caves
Men had inhabited
Since man was man.

Few can imagine
The wealth I squandered
Constructing the castle,
Nor the luck with which I prospered.

Soldiers walked the walls,
Spears and helmets
A second skyline. Ox-carts
Rumbled in the courts below.

Few can imagine
The ecstasies I tasted,
Bronzed men in the fields
Gathering crop on crop.

Even the sun,
Toiling like the rest,
Shoved its shoulder to the wheel
As the coffers filled.

The moon, too, grew cosy
In the dark stability of the towers,
As love succumbed
To the luxury of my purse.

But then the day
Dawned, in which money,
Like stones from the sky, smashed
My constructed castle.

Nor was it only revolution
But the relic I am
That even the guides to these ruins
No longer know my name.

A VISIT TO THE VILLAGE

We came, jostled in the back of a truck,
Five kilometres up the winding mountain road.
The village was deserted,
Except for a few chickens and an old woman
Pottering around a charred cauldron.

When we jumped out
Onto the cement square
By the war memorial,
We were laughing, I remember,
Sniffing the nostrils of our rifles
In the spring air.

The old woman
Gave us no bother.
We took over her house,
Uptilting litres of olive oil
Down our long throats.
But then our captain said
The men of the village had not surrendered
But scarpered to the scrub-oak.

This did not amuse us.
So we hunted them down
One by one, slaughtering them
In the mad mountains,
Killing the occasional fox
To underline our power.

A SIMPLE TWIST OF FATE

It was fun to begin with.
We made them undress,
Then poked the white flesh
With the nozzles of our machine-guns.

It wasn't much of a place,
A typical army barracks.
Bob Dylan was on the radio,
'Tangled up in Blue'.

When I had my idea,
The fun took off.
I wanted to degrade them
In their own eyes.

We laughed at how easy it was,
Fathers and sons castrating each other
With their teeth;
Prodded, of course, by our guns.

Then we shot them.
We all felt disgusted
To be in the presence
Of such a lack of self-respect.

All that was some time ago.
I live in the city now.
I've got a good job too
In the new car tax office.

KRISTEL

When we led her from the street
No one saw anything strange.
The people assumed
There was a bond between us.

She trotted along beside us
Chatting happily.
As for us, well,
Who could appear more normal?

The ascent up the mountain
Was, as usual, tedious.
We took it in turns
To hump the holy regalia.

We got her drunk that night,
Rolled up a little cannabis.
She lay down by the fire
Giggling herself to sleep.

We had already dug the grave
A week before we met her.
We lowered her gently in
Stroking her forehead.

As we cupped the earth in our hands,
Burying her alive,
We chanted the sacred words
From the printed book.

She had come along so peacefully,
Singing.
She was a stupid little thing.
At last we saw the sky

Exulting in the sun,
The blue purity of the dawn
The image of our land
Touched by the living god.

GO, GRACIOUS WORDS

Go, gracious words, go slaughter all you see
Slaughtering delight in one continual groan
From age to age: old age, the youthful bone
Now red with blood, now dead, with more to be.

Go, gracious words, go find the salty nurse,
Wiping the forehead on a screaming child
Heaved from the rubble, while the shells run wild,
Gracing the barrel of a sniper's curse;

Now taken out of time, pampered in my verse,
Pillowed in her bed, alive and well;
As, as we more suspect, in such a hell,
She's blown to bits in her bomb-exploded hearse.

Go, gracious words, inscribe in kingdom come
What ruin is, lies ruined, to blind and deaf and dumb.

II

The Light on the River

A MONK ARRIVES

Once more, thank God, a monk arrives,
The dada in our solemn lives.

CHURCH BELLS

Church bells ring in our sunny village,
This unfrequented part of the city.
Here, Sunday begins with a hope so palpable,
You can feel the horror of the times
Reaching back forever.

THE IRON GANG

Nine men were toiling on a lonesome road,
When one of them spoke up. He said, 'My load
Is heavy, brothers, heavier than I
Can bear. I think I'd rather die.'

The eight spoke softly in a neutral voice,
'It's death or this. You have a simple choice.'
'Simple I am not,' the man replied,
And giving up his toil, he gladly died.

AGAINST SERIOUSNESS

A young scholar sat in an orchard
Composing poetry on a serious theme.
All was well, until a friend said,
'Why do you annihilate existence?
This is the way to do it.'
And he danced under the apple trees
To a hidden music.

FÊTE

The blood rhythms of the bass guitar
Hallow the valley where the grapes hang green.
Clouds drift overhead. The sun-baked tiles
House the angles of mature enjoyment.

Scaffolding, cement-mixers, sand,
Stand idle, as hooters, bazookas, and the cries of girls
Intoxicate the rhythms, the rhythms,
The blood rhythms of the bass guitar.

PEOPLE

People are not so easy, you know.
They look easy, but they are not so.
Silly in T-shirts, asinine in shorts,
Christ approached these for his audience.

THE FRIEND WHO IS

Ah, the twinkling of the lights on Aëtos
Like a bracelet on my friend: bring to me
The friend who is, and not the mortal dross.

BOWLER HAT

Without wanting to, like a UFO,
I've followed this man's head
Through a day so tedious
I nearly took off on my own.

But then I saw the hat-peg
In the warm, suburban home,
His wife, the table laid, and a fire lit.
I'll stay, I thought, to check out the world.

POETRY

Not 'as it is', but blinding, like
Eros on a motorbike.

VEGA

Moon-mother, smaller than a moth,
You steady me, a drawing-pin
Holding up the map of the universe.

JUSTICE

Justice, with poets, is not found
In force, but in the purity of sound.

DOUBLE TAKE

There's another world mixed in with this one.
   You see it when someone dies.
The holy spirit of life and death
   And the monumental lies.

THE LIGHT ON THE RIVER

Don't come to me with your fascinating mind
   Fascinating me.
You see the way the light behaves on the river?
   That is the way to be.

III

In the Cradle of the Poets

IN THE CRADLE OF THE POETS

I pleasure long, I work to rule;
   Food and drink complete my day.
Is this a sin or wisdom? Who'll
   Cast the first stone on Conscience Day?
The nights are long with love and I'm
Between eternity and time.

I see her form forgive the grass
   On which she rests, her nakedness
Curved by the moon to a soft grace
   Not even I dare to address.
For as she moves, in outline, I
Witness the godliness of beauty.

Then dare I dare to speak, to feel
   The human engine in me start?
She shocks me with a shape so real
   Hers are the contours of my art,
Which, disembodied of my pain,
Distribute universal gain.

IN PRAISE OF PÉRIGORD

Douce land of grass and golden stone,
    Wide rivers, where the limestone caves
Reveal how hand of man alone
    Redeems how mind of man behaves,
Your forests, maize, tobacco, yield
Ten thousand sunflowers in a field.

We walk your treasury of trees
    Dappled by sunlight so serene
The wood-doves coo us to our ease
    Ensconced in soul-erupting green.
Before us, through your grassy banks,
    Winding like a silver road,
The Dordogne, image of a god,
    Distils our mortal thanks.

ST AGNE (IN DEFIANCE OF AN ABSTRACTION)

I feel comfortable in this village,
A man-atom in a soul-cleansing,
Drawing diagrams, doodling, marking time.
   What was the purpose of my life
Before I was born? Did the infinite
Spiral my being, like a mad
Astronaut, going nowhere, or did I
Have a purpose, before that gate-crashing?
   Here, in a green rain, where the trees
Drip their silver letters to the earth,
I engage with that Bastard-at-Arms,
Who, without flinch, torments me to this hour.
   Peace is the conquest of the evil powers
Both in the mind and in the fruity earth;
It is the richness of the buried vaults
Both in the mind and in the fruity earth.
   But time, without cessation, haunts me here,
Bending my purpose to its bitter will;
Yet I, conqueror of the man-atom I am,
Defy this foot-soldier of the infinite.
   Graceless, the infinite fingers me,
A simulacrum of true woman, even as she
Moves for my pleasure in her half-undress.
   Tormenting me will never do, my friend,
Though you are the infinite, I am human.
I see the fire, in its flames, contend
It would be, were it possible, human.
   So go, you Bastard, fuck off forever,
And leave me writing in this clement weather.

VISITATION IN THE MOUNTAINS

How will I forget
   Sitting there, unable to write,
The white page as blank
   As my mind concentrating
On nothing so successfully
   Nothing was written?

Painfully I coaxed
   Words from the music
I heard, out of reach,
   In the fluting of the mountain streams.
Yet every word was dead
   Because of my impatience.

To write, I learn, is to be wordless.
   The words arrive in their own way,
Like a party of unexpected friends
   In evening gowns and jokey tuxedoes
Sweeping up the hidden mountain track
   Giddy with wine and laughter.

A GLASS TO NATURE:
ON A FRIEND'S SIXTIETH YEAR

The shutters bang throughout the night.
The fir trees slap against the walls.
The moths attack the electric light.
The howling of the wind appals.

What can I say, dear Eddie, here
To help you through your sixtieth year?
I raise my unembittered glass
And watch the stormy fury pass.

You're getting on, my friend, and I
Level-peg with every hour.
Why should the lyric tongue be dry?
Or white hairs be the cause of fear?

I liked you young and like you now,
My one self-mocking sacred cow.
Dear Eddie, take these verses, say
The poetry your own sweet way.

NORMAN MacCAIG

He seemed, in the end, incorrigible.
A strange purpose drove him
As we struggled to understand.

There, in the moonlight, we saw him
Tampering with the construction of flowers
And the peculiar behaviour of words.

He was a poet, that much was clear.
But quite why he had to tamper
Was a question

The biographers of this Scottish poet
May never settle
As he tampers on and on.

My own opinion
From having known the man
Was that he could not see

How just because a grasshopper is known
By those who have known it,
It is a grasshopper. To be one, *he* had to be one.

DAUGHTER

Thirty summers have passed
Since I set eyes on your mother.
And yet, everywhere I go,
A faint aroma of how you were born

Perfumes my conscience.
For there, in the night,
As tender as we were,
She and I swung

In a hammock of consciousness
As you became yourself. Now you are young,
And take the beauty of ages in your arms,
Remember us, your parents, who gave you birth.

SPRING DAY NEAR REEPHAM

The hemlock hums, the wheat
   Rolls, rollicks, poppy-red.
A crow on crinkled feet
   Lands by the brood she bred.

In cloudless blue the moon
   Pins the sky at noon.
Two butterflies for hours
   Make love among the flowers.

Glittering, every bright
   Leaf on beech and birch
Transmits mosaic light
   Round the steeple on the church.

A WEEK IN THE COUNTRY

Soon we must be leaving.
   The pink sheets are folded
On the bed we may never see again.

The crocus in the barrel by the front door
   Breathes a yellow so radiant
We shall remember it

Long after the candlelit dinners,
   And what we said, are forgotten.
And surely, too, the robin,

Proud in his livery on the back lawn
   Under the pine trees, will brighten
The dark shadows which fall on our past.

So, until we leave, let us be living
   And loving, that our regret may be so intense
Happiness follows us like a faithful dog.

THE MYSTERY OF WINE

There are many intoxicants, and they all have their dangers.
But none is so intoxicating or dangerous, to my mind,
As the mystery of wine. This simple substance,
Taken in moderation, glorifies existence,
Gives understanding, makes us more kindly, and is
As near as dammit the vehicle of inspiration.

One thought troubles this neat arrangement.
What is moderation to one intoxicated with wine?

So, speaking of the dangers, there is the lure
Of wine as the secret accomplice of resentment.
We drink it, by the bucket, because it proves,
Mysterious as it is, we are the victims of life.

Between these two extremes, moderation stands
Directing the traffic of the busy city crossroads
        In the centre of my head.

IMMORTAL JELLYFISH

Lounging alone in my house one evening,
I walked out the front door
Because of the sound of nearby explosions.

Once outside, a glass of wine in my hands
Reflecting the light of the lamp over the doorway,
I saw the fireworks erupting, two streets away,

As the shiver of renewal elbowed my idleness.
Suddenly the night, ponderous with thunderclouds,
Reclined like a body as the rockets

Pierced to the heart of its now discerned desire.
One more stunned than happy, I lay on the grass,
My back against the wall, sipping the wine,

As rocket after rocket strained to achieve its union;
Exploding, one by one, to create, in the heavens,
Immortal jellyfish, the last singeing my lawn.

A SEALED BOX FOR XANTHI

In many years from now, you'll read
These lines I write, when I am dead.
Why were you born, my darling, or
What is a person living for?

Let us assume these questions are
One question, all-the-more bizarre:
How should we approach this life,
Which murders us, the more we love?

In lines of love I have before
Written more,
Which I perceive small use to you, as you
Do what you do.
How may the music of my mind inspire
In you, who played with me for hours,
The living fire,
When all that's left of me is flowers?

Your life ago, the light of dawn
Shone in your eyes, five minutes born.
You had a look of fiery pride
In which my egotism died.

When you were one, or two, or three,
You had the measure of my heart;
And long before I could devise
A way for me
To instruct you in the art
Of being alive, you were heavenly-wise,
Drinking
Through a straw,
Conscious of compassion as a primary choice, a decision,
Which you enacted with precision,
And set me thinking.
And then I saw
Love precedes what we are living for.

Do you remember how we made a rocking-horse
Out of rubbish?
How you swung, in a swish, swish, swish,
An original emblem of the force
By which such love is known?
I rock you in the bone.
To have had such moments with you is bliss
Conscious of the kiss
With which we leave
This earth, on which we quarrel, love, and grieve.

IV

Bestial

SOW

Grumpy old thing, you chew
A lump of coke
By the back door.

How serene you are
Splayed in your pen,
Your head on a pillow of straw,

As eight pink nuzzlers
Draw from the core of your being
The milk of motherhood.

PIGLET

Snugger than joy
Your ruby snout
Rubs the trough
Of my iron hand.

On your back
I stroke the white bristles
Dearer to me
Than mink.

Go now and run
About the house
Believing in it
As I do.

MOORHEN

Like a mad cowboy with a red-hot iron
Branding the earth with symbols of ownership,
You print the muddy edges of the river.
Toasting-forks! What are they?
Is this the imprimatur of a serious bird?

FLY

Like a critic, your thousand-sided eyes,
Your winged back, your well-prepared mouth,
Hunt the food of poetry
Inexhaustibly.

BUTTERFLY

Sunlight bloomed in the garden
As the shadows of the buildings
Posited the laws of artistic perspective.
Then, out of a bush, a butterfly
Ruined them all in a chaos of yellow.

MANDRIL

Red-nosed lord of the jungle night,
Speak to me. Only the yellow-green of your eyes
Answers, as I flash alive
To the unspeakable dignity of the beast.

MOVING HOUSE

You lie on the grass
Serenely, on your back,
The white hoops of your ribs
Visible below your bra-line.

Who is more stunned,
You or I,
To see you knee-jerk upwards,

Now a column of ants,
With eggs in their legs,
Passes under you,
Moving house?

SOLOIST

Distinguished among the green, the cabbage-white
Butterfly butterflies over the lawn,
As the enormous orchestra of the afternoon
Listens to the soloist of silence.

HUNTING OWL

As it is, true silence reigns.
    The borealis tints the night.
The moon invades my windowpanes
    And checks the floor with light.

No hunting owl corrects my thought
    But flies it to a spinney nest
Where skinny wings lie curled and taut
    And eloquence is brought to rest.

HEIFER

Elegant the heifer to whose nose
The tender roots' aroma blows.

PIKES

The stream ran down to the river,
But at its top was a pool
In which we played, when young.

Too important now
For what we had outgrown,
We set out for the river.

We all recall the sunlight cascading
On the torrential rush of events
As we hit the new water

And felt the shock
Of the electric bliss of freedom.
Then we saw the pike

Hanging in the water,
Its fins both down-playing and encouraging
Malice aforethought.

Surely it was strange
As we turned to each other
And recognised ourselves.

V

A Love Song to Eros

I SAW HIM IN MY SLEEP LAST NIGHT

I saw him in my sleep last night.
    Again my fever grew
To such a fever pitch I tried
    To murder you.

I stabbed you through the heart and stared
    Directly in your eyes.
The blood was brimming on my hands,
    Yet you arose.

The spirit of your pity pressed
    Your features on the air.
You watched me on that bleeding bed
    The pain endure.

Who loves another, loves a ghost.
    We shared the rattling chain.
Now all we had is dead or lost,
    We tug it on, alone.

Love, love, love, love, love, love, love,
    Seven times hoops the brain,
A ditched, dyked fortress set to brave
    The starry armies come.

And I will love you till each star
    Flakes in the crystals of our eyes,
And each perceives our courts of war
    Arch wysteria and rose.

DALLIANCE

Love is a dalliance, they say.
A dalliance? As when two scorpions
Are momentarily civil to each other?
Nonsense! Love is a force
Which separates lover from lover,
As in the Tantric and Taoist art
In which sexual congress
Is maintained
Indefinitely.

PICNIC

On the bank of a river
Under a flamboyance of poplars
We lay in one another's arms,
The debris of our picnic all around us.

Over our faces, over the poplars, but under
The blue, a cloud containing existence
Is a white, slow-moving barge
Made weightless by our happiness.

ENTENTE CORDIALE

The way your neck increases rash desire
Would make an honest man an honest liar.

Your upcurled hair, the wild bits hanging down,
Mark where a married man begins to drown.

MEMO

It's a brief, a very brief song.
If you're in love, in love,
Fucking another is wrong.

A GAME OF CROQUET

Her body, a croquet mallet,
Hits my hope
Through the hoop. Suddenly
I am an English afternoon
With nothing further to enjoy
Than a glass of Pimm's,
And her eyes, like an ocelot's,
Thwacking me through the hoops of reason.

PERFECT FORM

How shall I achieve the perfect form, I thought,
As my content lay on her back
With her legs open.
Love, she said, is the perfect form of content.

HOMELIFE STUDY

More studied than the light
Which beats through my doorway,
You are the curves of thought
As the decanter fills.

Under your tutelage
The sun, too, aspires
To the curves of thought, with which you
Entrance me.

Endlessly fascinating,
You heave
The hills of thought
Into the anatomy of your body.

A man alive
To the ecstasy of being,
I read your nakedness
As a man re-enters paradise.

MUSE

Go. I cannot bear
   To look at you,
So perfect I must throw
   The book at you.

Stay. I do not dare
   To berate you,
Couched, naked, free, the way
   I create you.

STRIKE THE LOVELY DUMB

Strike the lovely dumb, be curt with praise.
This lady is no incident so vain.
She wears the long-time miracle, she stays,
For in my heart I feel dissolving pain.

Wonders of love, raptures of love, dear God,
Queue at the shop where I barter words for her;
For she, Christ's child, has brains no brain has made
Approving commerce Godly words concur.

In California now dark streets appraise
Her lone eyes looking from a window there
Screening a dream no Hollywood would dare.

For on the Pacific moonlight softly strays
Trembling with language on her parting lips
As out of clothes into these words she slips.

UNDONE BY LOVE

Undone by love, by love I am undone.
At first the school, in which we fall in love
And see a radiance in a friendly face
Cool to a stranger whom we wish to shun.

Next the bed, where learning what's above
And what's below, reveals this state of grace
Rots to a rut in which we crawl apart
Chained to a ball of money, our children in tears.

Next, disenfranchised with a broken heart,
We risk the rocks, the cynics' prey, to find,
Suicidal nihilists in a double-bind,
Love is nothing, and nothing as it appears.

And this is why, my spider's net now spun,
Undone by love, by love I am undone.

DRINKING SONG

Lower your eyelids. Lift your glass.
   Raise it with your eyes.
Look at me. Look at me. All things pass
   But none so witty or wise.

The truth (it's immortal) wears your smile
   Whenever you smile at me.
So raise your glass, your eyes, and I'll
   Toast to the truth I see.

Drinking and happy and halfway drowned
   In bottomless glasses of wine,
Let's celebrate the truth of our state:
   I'm yours and you are mine.

A LOVE SONG TO EROS

You're a smasher and a smiler and a triple turning dive,
The somersaulting intellect inside the thing alive.
You duck, and twist, and toss, and swim the raging sea,
A finger in my mind, like a spoon in tea.

There's murder in the boardroom, death in every nerve,
The evil get more evil and what the good deserve.
Rape, starvation, age and pain, sorrow and disease,
And people pray to you, dear god, the all-time tease.

You're a honey in the morning. You're never twice the same.
There's not a soul I know to hope to scandalize your name.
Let's have a drink beside the fire. I'll walk you down the street.
We'll split up by the water-wheel and swear we'll never meet.

We'll meet of course tonight and feel the tender spark
Illuminate our loving in the blissful dark.

VI

The Dancing Crocodile

GRIEF

Ablaze with grief
I used to sit
In the tired anatomy
Of my understanding.

Bodily decrepitude
Dragged me under.
The soul of reason
Was a poisoned chalice.

All year the river
Wound without meaning,
Meandering onwards
To a futile sea.

Grief, I learnt slowly,
Is a furtive burning,
In which the brow of a midge
Is first noticed.

BEING HERE. TWO POEMS FOR ADAM JOHNSON (1965-93)

1

No one could agree
Why the leaves were falling.
Nor to what purpose
Yellow, red, or brown.

The arguments grew heated
In the marble schools,
As thunder overhead,
On bright spikes of lightning,

Tumbled into snow.
Now the lingerie of sleep,
Whiter than a sheet,
Lingers on the trees.

Too soon, too soon, we wake.
No deeper than our dreams,
The snow-drop and the rose
Caress us into time.

2

Never again, dear Adam, never again the sun
Exploding on a washing-up bowl. All that is done.
Never again red wine, the white bow-tie,
The evenings behind the bar at P.E.N., the wry

Jokes with strangers in the afternoon pubs.
Never again, one hopes, the literary snubs.
Never again your wolf-like smile, your view
Of all I see now, a sky of spotless blue.

A prism swings in the house. Its rainbow
Reminds me of what the mournful know:
The sweetness, the sweetness of life,
Has cast you from it. And this is why I grieve.

The truth is this simple. I grieve to see
Never again, never again will you be.

THE CAUSE

They say you should have been more careful
With the way you ordered your life. Easy for them,
You reply, your voice still alive, as you search

For why you died so young. Only your mother,
Suspecting your death was not so simple,
Spotted the cause in the vegetation of the mind.

For there, like a hyena, laughing without vengeance,
She saw the cause, once again on the prowl,
As the pundits slept, crunch you in its jaws.

More alive than a beast, it ate up your life,
And some of theirs as well, as the foolish stars
Reasoned, to no purpose, their infinite logic.

THE WICKED CORKSCREW

Because I could not achieve
The music I had set myself to compose,
The wicked corkscrew
Came to the aid of my silence.

By night in the bars I watched it
Sucking out the blocks in my body,
As the music of my companions
Sounded on the mirrored walls

All I was feeling. Dead drunk, I stumbled
Home to my faithful lover, all my dreams
Slumped in the sack I was, as I lay on his doorstep.
Patient as ever, he dragged me in by the ankles.

All that has ended now. I'm on my own,
The wicked corkscrew alone
The champion of my abilities.
Oh hear how the corks are popping, as they lower me in.

REMORSE

    A cold wind lashes the empty street.
        Darkness covers the town.
    Twenty years to achieve defeat
        Of my dreams come tumbling down.

    Nowhere alive the self-same heart
        That I in the battle won.
    Nowhere alive the imaginative part
        Of my mind when I begun.

    All is stale and old and worn
        And the wind goes whistling by.
    Who will reveal how a song is born
        In the light of a poet's eye?

    I was alive when worlds were wrought
        In the white of a sun's design.
    Now all I feel is the chill of thought
        In this cold little room of mine.

    Gone is the grace of a generous mind
        And a heart that walked through hell.
    Now all I know are the scurrilous kind
        And their politics as well.

    Down from the sky comes the kiss of night
        And up from the floor the same.
    I curse the day when I first saw light
        And thought of a poet's fame.

    I sold my soul to the devils of drink
        And my heart to the whores of gold.
    Now every time I think I think
        I feel my blood run cold.

    I should have listened to the ones before
        Who knelt where I'm kneeling now,
    And learnt how the mighty atoms roar
        And stuck to my poet's vow.

THE THIN END OF THE WEDGE

There was no way forward.
There was no way back.
I sat at my desk
With nothing but time

Ticking on my wrist-watch.
Into the blankness
Came a thought
Like the toe of a stranger

In a long-unvisited house.
'What do you want?' I said,
Expecting no solace
From such an intruder.

'I am the wedge,' the thought informed me,
'Driving into your brain.
You will feel nothing at first,
But slowly you will see

Time split apart, the past and the future
No longer relevant, as the
Ticking of your watch becomes
Geared to the nucleus.'

I was not amused,
Until the thought
Drove into me, all the way home.
'What now?' I laughed,

Creation all around me
An imminent possibility only.
'Shall I create the world?
Or shall I let it

Remain uncreated?' I heard
The question clearly enough,
As the thought withdrew from my head
Like an axe of light.

SISTER

After a decade or two
Getting none the wiser,
I saw the coffin
Of my dearly-belovéd
Sister
Lowered into the earth.

We used to play
All day.
When we were older
We grew bolder.

When did it start,
The blip in your heart?
Why did you die?
I

Pray all day,
Older and bolder,
My sweet decay
On so strong a shoulder.

THE WILD MEN

The wild men are back.
Those witty and chummy guys
Are back. And what a vengeance of pleasure
They exact in the village square
They cemented into place.

The wild men are drinking.
Dancing breaks out under the eucalyptus trees.
The young women clap their hands
As ferocious explosions
Remind the old of the wars.

The wild men are laughing
Because they build the place,
The very church, in which the wise
Conduct the order of religion.

The wild men want no peace.
Peace brought them poverty.
What they want
Are the orgies of rock and roll
Blotting out the squalor of their lives.

And so it comes
Out of the ghetto-blaster
Under the bunting and over their grandmothers' cakes,
The squalor of rock and roll
In which I delight.

THE SAGE OF THE CAMBRIAN MOUNTAINS

Tramp the hills, old sage, the chapel there
Is stones the rains now whip with merciless
Lashes. The mortar's all dissolved. Once sacred air
Now kills the strong foundations where you learnt to bless.

There's nothing left. The hills are lost in rain.
The antique yew lies rotting in the grass.
The flaking graves say nothing about pain.
There's nothing left. And nothing, too, will pass.

Slowly the clouds co-operate with night
To freeze the lakes. The winds do not relent.
This is the way of life. And it is right
You tramp the hills, old sage, with sage intent.

Blitzed by the blizzard, long morning helps you stand
Snowy-haired in snow, with one uplifted hand.

THE DANCING CROCODILE

Serious men were appalled
When the sky split
And the dancing crocodile appeared
On the stage of the horizon.

All day in the sun,
As we gazed anxiously on our flocks,
The crocodile danced on its tail
With a diamond smile in its eyes.

Some were charmed, but the majority
Scoffed at the beast, retiring
To shelter, not quite convinced
It was, or was not, there.

And then we saw it
Pirouette, more and more brazenly,
As the sinking sun adorned it
In a thousand hues.

In such a dusk we lost it,
Until we saw the diamonds
Blinking once again, moving towards us
Through the river of night.

Spinning in a wild
Ecstasy, it gobbled,
One by one, the stars
And the innocent moon.

Serious men recall
No more memories
Of how we were consumed
Nor came to life.

THE BALLAD OF HUMAN SACRIFICE

I came to a place where many had been before.
Footprints dented the sand as far as the eye could see.
But no one was there. I hoiked a fallen deck-chair upright
And sat gazing on a tranquil bay. The sun set

Like a perfect circle investigating a straight line.
When darkness and cold finally overcame me,
I drove back to where I had come from,
And poured myself a glass of wine, puzzling

At the disappearance of the many people
Who had witnessed the miracle I had been denied.
Dreaming that night, I saw a village square
Buzzing with people and the rumours of a god;

And knew at once that I was to be satisfied.
Coming down from the church, the man leading the file
Held his own son before him on his outstretched arms.
'Behold my son!' he cried, 'Behold my son!'

And so I did. And the miracle was this:
Though killed in a fit of religious passion,
A sacrifice to any god there might be,
His son was not only alive but unharmed.

We witnessed this. The young man in his father's arms,
Naked and breathing, had not a scratch on him.
When I awoke, I went back to the beach
As the sun was rising. And there were the footprints

Unruffled by even a feather of wind.
Turning it to the east, I sat in the deck-chair
And saw Christ cross-legged on the sun holding the straight line
Of the horizon, which he drew up with him

Till brightness covered the world and the time was nine.
Now skewered to my deck-chair, but not wanting to
Miss a moment of this miraculous happening,
I took out my notebook and pencil and spoke to him.

I said, 'Why have all the people disappeared?'
'They haven't, nor is there any witness except yourself.
For these are the many times,' he continued, pointing to the footprints,
'When you came to worship at the altar of forgiveness.'

'It wasn't me.' I said, scribbling down his words
As fast as I could, 'This is my first time here,
If you include last night.' 'Not so. For consider this:
You are the prototype of many. Forgive me,

For I know you are only a common sinner,
But didn't you dream last night about a
Human sacrifice in which a young man was unhurt?'
'I did.' 'That was me. You heard my father cry out.

And now, on the beach, my question to you is
Will you forgive the evil within yourself
Which will not forgive evil? Please think before you speak.'
My soul, I saw, was at stake, and I myself

Was lighting the kindling under my evil form.
Did I light the flames of heaven or of hell?
Did I choose evil? Or did I choose to forgive
The evil within me, which was within my reach?

'I am on your side,' I said, 'I choose forgiveness.'
'A warrior defending it with your life,'
He added, dissolving into the sun
Now blazing alone in the cloudless sky

And a commonplace afternoon. I drove my car
Back to the place from which I had come,
And poured myself a glass of wine, puzzling
At the terror in the world because of free choice.

THE RATCHET EFFECT

Sweet, without interview, our love affair
Marries the downthrust of the sun
On a rented farmhouse to the care
With which we do the difficult doing, done.

Not to achieve is fine. But to achieve
The ribald chatting with the philosophic
Is fate on fire. The poems which we leave
Seem less manual than automatic.

Done to keep breathing, the poems hold their own
Against comparison with a farmer's chores.
He comes and goes, bone on whitened bone,
As we do too, in union with the stars.

And in our art, I see ourselves made sane,
The past made present, the future future gain.